MR. STRONG

By: Alex Tilley

To my girls, Chantal and Natalie.

To Chris, Landon, James, Blair, & Kyle.

To black hair and dark eyes,

Pale skin and snake smiles.

1

Not too tall. Not too wide. A refined mass like a sharpened topaz. Elgan flexed at himself in the mirror. Any addiction that made someone look and feel as good as he did was bound to be worth it. He was dense and toned. He bounced his pecs then snorted at his lack of modesty. He released his flex and questioned his boxer's bulge. It looked lumpy. He finished dressing. He shouldered his duffle bag and left the gym. The sun was rising.

The sidewalks were vacant. Coffee shops were the only windows of light in the dim blue. Early commuters lined the drive-throughs. The morning energy invigorated him. He felt the pleasurable tightness of the fresh pump in his arms, as he turned into his driveway.

He sat down in the front inside stairway and pulled off his shoes with the groans befitting a good workout. A new day's quiet was painted on the walls. He popped a pod into the coffeemaker and turned it on. He walked to the fridge and grabbed the shake he had made in advance. He drank it with subdued distaste and placed the cookies and cream powder-stained flagon in the sink. He checked the oven's green digital clock. He had thirty-minutes until work. He rushed upstairs and dressed, ran back downstairs, grabbed his coffee, then got in his car. He backed out his driveway with his swollen arm heavy on the passenger headrest.

A sycophant, a slave, a sold soul: they all passed him in a slumped forward duty to the road. He droned as one of them until a wall of red eyes halted in a sway. He slammed the break to the floor. His body snapped like a whip. The sound of crunching crackled in his ears. Just like that, he knew the day was a write off.

"Sir, are you okay?" a woman asked from the edge of his shattered passenger window.

He blinked and breathed. His chest still felt the pulsations of his morning workout. He felt the calluses of his hands against the leather steering wheel.

"Yeah... Yes, I'm fine. No – What? I'm good... I'm good. Thanks. Just give me a minute and I'll get my information for you," Elgan said shakily.

"Sir, are you sure?" the woman leaned into the window. "You've got blood coming down your forehead."

"Oh, I–"

"Hey, is everyone alright?" a man asked, as he stepped beside the woman.

"Yeah, I'm–"

"Holy shit! I'm gonna call 9-1-1. What's your names?" a voice called out.

"Michelle, uh, Michelle G-Goswami. I don't know his name... He looks disoriented," the woman hummed.

"Sir – Sir, you okay? Are you okay?" a muffled voice asked.

"Yeah, I'm fine. My name is, uh, Elgan. Elgan... Elgan Bluffs."

Elgan heard the sound of voices, but they were out of focus.

"Hey, you should probably just sit there until the ambulance shows up." A man reached into the car through the broken window and turned his ignition off.

Elgan went to push the hand away, but he couldn't move. He didn't feel any pain, he didn't even feel his pump, but he couldn't lift his arm. He couldn't move his gripped hands from the wheel.

"Listen, I - I think something's wrong. I can't move. I can't move my arms. I - What the fuck is going on? Help me up. Can you help me up?"

The man backed away, repulsed.

"No one touch him. I think we should wait for an ambulance." The man was frantic.

"Don't listen to this guy... Help me out. Help me out, please!" Elgan begged. "What's wrong with you people?" He couldn't feel the relief of his breaths and began to breathe faster. He couldn't feel his chest. A sharp tingle prickled off his calloused fingers. He wanted to pinch himself. His body ached from the suspension of feeling. Something trickled over his eye and into his mouth: blood. "What happened? What's wrong with me?"

"Hey, everyone okay?" another voice asked.

"I can't move! I can't move," Elgan called to them. The voices pulled further and further away. He could barely hear them. Everything seemed discoloured in the blur of his consciousness. Everything was in a haze. "I can't feel anything. Oh shit... Oh shit..."

"Did someone call 9-1-1!" a person yelled.

"Call 9-1-1. Call 9-1-1. Call 9-1-1," Elgan cried. "Oh fuck - call 9-1-1. Please. Please."

He heard car horns and a thumping bass. He heard asinine chatter and whiny complaints. He heard a popping exhaust. The noise gripped him by the throat. Life was consumed in a swirling mechanical collapse of harmony, and his eyelids closed desperately on his ears' behalf. He could still hear the noise in the darkness.

2

The pitter-patter of rain on the window kept Elgan's breathing in focus. Each exhalation exhausted from his lips as he sought a rhythm. He wanted to yell to his mom for tea, but breathlessness stayed his hand. He listened to the rain instead. Raleigh was on his mind. He hadn't seen her in years. Had it already been years? The thought of her made him smile. Smile. Smile. He realized his hand was gripped. His uncut nails left indents in his palms.

"Smile. It's okay to smile. It's okay to smile. She would want us to smile, wouldn't she?" he coached in whispers to himself.

He had to smile. He tried to hold on to it, but it was nothing more than raindrops down glass. He tried to flex his pecs to remind himself that he was still a man, but they were motionless in his bed-ridden decline.

He heard a knock on his door and the nasal clearing of his dad on the other side.

"You alright in there, bud? I'm off to work. Let me know if you need anything," his dad said without opening the door.

Elgan didn't answer. He thought of the responses that were expected, but he let the silence mask his awareness. He heard the creak of his dad's steps as he walked away.

Elgan looked at the white stucco ceiling then summoned the will to stand and walk to his closet mirror. An ugly stranger stared back at him. His large shoulders were unsightly with his declining arms. His lined abs were a lined gut. His pecs were boobs. He walked to his dresser and pulled last night's t-shirt from the top. He slipped on slippers out of routine and left his room for the toilet.

He saw his mom working at the table as he walked past the kitchen to the washroom. He heard her fingers clicking off her laptop keyboard as he pissed. He finished and went to wash his hands but caught his own sunken eyes in the mirror. Eyes like a stoner. Glazed and tight with deep purple bags. He couldn't help but stare. He ran his hand through his hair, but it flopped back down like a straw toupee. He grabbed the razor at the side of the sink and shivered at the rusted blades. He wanted to know if he could do it. He somehow knew he could but put it back down and walked to the kitchen.

"Hey," his mom said without looking up at him, "there's not much in the cupboards. Do you want to walk to the store later to grab some groceries for me?"

"Come on, you know I can't," he said, annoyed that she would even ask.

He grabbed a half-eaten bag of chips from the top of the fridge and walked back to his bedroom.

Rain still ran down his room's window. He sat at the edge of the bed and ate handfuls of chips without thought. He wiped the chip dust from his fingers on his shirt then grabbed the phone that was tucked under his pillow. He threw it back down as he realized it had nothing of relevance. Vapid displays of enslaved round-hipped nothingness and politics of fear and hate. AI driven drivel. He looked at the weights on the floor and felt his own vapid irrelevance. He wanted to do something with himself but felt the hopelessness of each thing he picked up. He sat at the edge of the bed like a c-shaped slug. He looked at his fingernails. He couldn't recall the last time he cut them. Raleigh used to tell him that the most unattractive thing in her mind was dirt under long fingernails, but why that memory spanned time was unbeknownst to him. He brought his knees to his chest. He saw himself in the closet mirror and shook his head. There was a strange creature side-eying him. He stood up quickly and grabbed the weights. He had to get a few curls in.

He pumped them. He tried to focus on his muscles. He put them down slowly then breathed deeply. He was a pitiful child. He could curl more than that when he was twelve. He picked them up again and curled them until the strain popped vessels in his face. He dropped them then paced with the energy of testosterone raging inside of him. He wasn't a slug. He was a man. He tried to flex at himself and shook his head. He breathed aggressively then picked the weights from the floor and curled them twice and clunked them down with pride. He wanted to do more, but he didn't want to overdo it. He quickly tried another quick flex, sighed, and then grabbed a pair of boxers and a towel for a shower.

He was left flaccid when he discovered the bathroom door closed and locked.

"How long you going to be?" he asked through the door.

"Just give me a few minutes," his mom said, annoyed that her privacy had been tainted.

"Okay, just let me know when you're done," he sighed.

He walked back to his room and grabbed his phone. By the time his mom yelled down the hall that she was done, he was tossing his phone to the floor in his numbed shame.

He showered quickly, finding no comfort in the tepid water. He let himself drip onto the carpet as he stared into the clouded mirror. He saw a shade. A mist born creature with splotches of red maiming its skin. He couldn't help but look at the rusted blades of the razor again, erect like a high-browed second lieutenant from RMC. He slapped it off the counter then found his way back to the edge of his bed where he sat silently in a state of self-mutilating reflection.

He could hear the beating of his pulse in his head. The *thup thup* made him want to cry. *Thup thup, thup thup,* like a leaking faucet. He had to leave. He had to go somewhere. He threw on clothes, grabbed his phone and keys, then was on his hands and knees looking for his wallet. He wanted to scream. The *thup thup* was like a blockage in his ears. He tripped over a small pile of unwashed clothes and cracked his knee off the corner of the bed. The collision was reverberating, but he stood without pain.

The wallet on the desk's top immediately caught his attention. He scooped it up shamelessly, threw on a jacket, and found relief from the *thup thup* as the sound of rain splashing off the earth replaced it.

3

The rain's untainted music brought life to the early March slush that piled up against curbs like the bodies of the washed-up homeless. It's splashing sang in calming psalms. It reminded Elgan of the water that dripped from the baptised. Raleigh probably would have liked him to be baptised. Instead, she got a cripple.

He walked the deserted block to the store. He tried not to look into the windows of other people's homes, but the daytime dimness made it easy to catch a glimpse into secret worlds. He had a deep longing to see what people did with their time when no one was watching, but he resisted it.

He walked past a park with some teenagers and tried not to focus on their deviance. He could feel their eyes following him in a strange interpre-tation of their own guilt or malevolence.

"Hey, sir!" one called out. The pack of them approached him like Badlands hyenas. "Sir, would you like to buy some chocolate? We're selling it for our school." The smallest of their group smoked a sloppy joint. A cloud of the marijuana smoke puffed out of his nostrils. "We've got some green too, if you're interested?"

"No, I'm good. Thanks guys," Elgan said. He tried to turn away, but he was pulled back.

"You sure? We can see that bulge in your back pocket. You don't have a couple bucks for a chocolate bar? It's for a good cause. Cancer or some shit," the leanest of the boys said. He seemed tall for a teenager.

"Nah man, I'm good. I'll see if I'm interested on my way back though. Thanks," Elgan said amiably. He looked down at the hand on his wrist. "You going to let go of me or what?"

They all laughed. Elgan looked at their peach fuzz faces. He tried to rip his hand away, but the boy held it with the desperation of social pressure. Elgan gripped the boy's wrist and twisted it off his own. The boy grunted as Elgan shoved him away.

"Hey, what the hell are you doing?" the lean

boy demanded. They circled in tighter. They looked more and more unpredictable.

"You tried to break my arm, asshole," the boy he shoved whined, bracing his own wrist.

"What's wrong with you, man?" another boy said. Elgan began to lose track trying to watch them all. They shuffled in closer. He could sense them shifting nervously as they all began to chide him. They stank like weed. Rain patted off their mopped heads.

He saw a quick movement in his peripherals and tried to swipe it away. They all stepped back as he pulled his swinging arm back from a bared knife. Blood ran off his hand like spilling paint. It dripped on his shoes and fed the earth with the rain. The boy with the knife shakily stepped forward again. He looked confused.

"What the hell are you doing?" the boy demanded. He kept the blade angled towards Elgan's stomach. "G - give us your wallet! Give us your money. Or - or - I'll fucking stab you again. Come on!"

Elgan stared at the blood flowing out of him. Something about the painlessness pissed him off. He grabbed the kid by the neck and shoved him away.

The boy slipped on the wet grass and fell backwards. The knife flew out of the boy's hand as he fell, but he scrambled for it like a fish squirming on wet rocks. The others watched him with open mouths, frozen like trolls caught in the daylight. Elgan stepped forward. He tried to staunch the seeping flow with his other hand, but it leaked out from beneath his palm. He stomped on the slipping boy's head, picked up the knife, looked at the wide-eyed pack around him, then speed-hobbled back home.

4

Elgan crept with dripping impunity to the washroom. Would his mother even notice the mess? He was dripping like a stuck pig. He started the shower and soaked the base of the tub orange as the blood poured out of the slice in his arm. Almost mugged by children. Kids. He wondered if he had been a piece of shit like them when he was their age? Or was the generational violence, angst, and sexual desperation a genetic disposition?

He quickly compressed the spilling wound, dripped to the sink, flung open the bottom cabinet, and grabbed the first aid kit. He put his arm under the water to wash it of the dripping juices, then wrapped the gauze around it in tight loops. He found a safety pin and clipped the gauze snug. He dried himself and threw on boxers, socks, a sweater, and jeans and went for his room, but his mom was coming down the hallway. Her hair was wrapped in a bun, and she was looking down at her phone.

"You showering again?" she asked.

"Yeah, I slipped when I was outside, so I figured I should wash myself off," he said.

"Ahh, okay. Be careful. Let me know if you need anything, I'm just going to lie down. Caroline has been dreadful today, and I just need a break, a real break break. Working like this is going to kill me young... Did you grab everything from the list while you were out?" Her tired eyes watched him.

"I, uh, I didn't end up getting there - to the store that is. After I fell, I kind of just came right home." He could sense the distrust in her gaze.

"Okay, honey. I was planning on going out anyway." She walked past him. Her shoulders seemed pulled down by the exhaustion that bagged her eyes.

He walked quickly to his room, shut the door, and locked it. He paced. The frightened eyes of the boy with the knife watched him from his mind. The boy had felt the wrath of power in a fire's spark; blown out in a slipping miscalculation. Elgan had captured that spark in his soul. He caught himself in the mirror and realized he was hard as a rock. He could've done more. He would've done more. He should've done more. Excitement shivered through him in a forgotten sensation. He looked at his hands. They were warm. They shook. His toes suddenly felt the warmth of life. He touched himself. He pulled his hand away with a shuddering gasp. Sensation pulsed through him. Heat like a microwaved glass bowl. Pain followed. His brain grew wild with excitement as the sensations began to blur his vision. He fell backwards onto his bed. He could feel the thumping relief of his shoe against the boy's head like popping bubble wrap. He needed it again. He laughed with orgasmic jubilation as the muscles in his face crinkled unexpectedly. His tongue felt wet and lustful. He stretched and tensed his arms and legs with an explosive release.

He stumbled off the bed. He was on his knees as the pulsing burned in his veins. He dragged himself to his chair. Each pulse like a murmur in his heart, catching his breath and freezing him in a moment of realized mortality. His chest seemed burdened by the release. The blinking spots shifted in drunken spins. He heard knocking. Knuckles knocking in reluctant obligation of concern. He understood.

"I'm going out, Elgan," his mom called through the door. He could barely hear her through the pulsations in his head. Her words may as well have been coming from the moon.

"Okay!" he heard himself call back, an echo of a voice that he knew was his and hated.

The colours from his Marilyn Manson poster were speckled in his vision. He felt high. Higher than life. Floating. He could probably fly with the energy that pulsated from his being. Instead, he curled closer into himself. Childish grins drooled like snarling beasts around him. He heard their laughter, then he remembered their fear.

He stood up with destabilising vibrations, a calf's first steps. He walked slowly to the door and whipped it open. He was thankful his parents set him up in the spare bedroom on the first floor, as he walked with less stability than an old, married tradesman on a Friday night.

He stumbled to the family room. He looked out the front window. His mom's car was already gone. He went to return to his room, but the pulsating began to calm. His old strength of life began to slip away. He fell onto the couch gripping his chest. His breathing was sharp and frightening. The room darkened. He could no longer tell if he was blinking or staring lifelessly into nothingness.

5

Elgan had dreamt, but he hadn't remembered any of it.

It was dark and quiet. His fan's absence was audible. Sweat dribbled off his eyelash. He slipped his socks off with his toes.

What a man to be curled onto his parent's couch like a decrepit mongrel. He was once a man, he thought. A bull. It never mattered how thin his hair was, women and men saw his traps, his bis, and his quads. A swollen beast. All that remained now was a body of shoestring limbs and imagined fantasies of feeling while lying on his parents' faux-leather couch. Moneyless. Jobless. A body without soul. A heart without life.

He pulled up his sleeve and looked at his wrapped arm. The bandage had darkened. He pulled his sleeve back down and struggled weakly to his feet.

He walked to the kitchen and grabbed a glass of water. The glow of the digital clock from the oven provided enough light for him to manoeuvre without tripping. He took his glass back to the front window. His mom's car and his dad's truck were in the driveway. He stared at them. The outside light glared off the truck's driver door, spotlighting it for him. He pulled his eyes away from it and sat back down where he had been lying. He drank the water with the absence of satisfaction he was used to. He didn't even know why he drank it.

He sat there in the silence and then twisted to look out the window again. Somehow, he felt watched. He brought his eyes to the hedge at the edge of the sidewalk and stared motionlessly. He tried not to blink and have the watcher slip away without him seeing. He questioned his reasoning for blinking. He stared. Nothing. A standard display of his being: nothing. Not even fear filled the void. Feelingless nothing.

He walked to the front door and stepped outside. The slushy suburban street was cast in the shadows left between the streetlight spotlights. He walked to the store. His bare feet stopped when they reached the park. The grass had a moist sheen where the streetlights hit it. He tried to find the spot where the boys attacked him, but he quickly realized the futility of his search. He turned to go back home but felt a need to make his mark somewhere. He channelled the spirit of his mongrel depravity and pissed on the playground's slide. He laughed. He couldn't stop laughing. He screamed with laughter. His shoulders jumped up and down in his body's effort to support the release. He felt trapped by it. He saw lights in windows flick on, and the shades of spying figures peek out at him. He just laughed more.

A car pulled up. He saw the word police undulate in the light. A cop with a tactical light stepped out and walked toward him. The light's whiteness blinded him.

"Then, brothers, it came. Oh, bliss, bliss and heaven," he called out.

"Hey, you alright?" the glow retorted.

"You here to take me in?" Elgan asked, strangely nervous.

"I'm just here to check on a noise complaint, sir." The light swivelled and passed over the park. It searched the ground and shot quickly back to Elgan. "Are you alone here, sir? It's quite late." The cop's other hand slid like a stalking viper to something buckled in her vest.

"I'm sorry... I was just going to the store. I'm a little...disoriented," he said. His mind spoke on his behalf. "I'm not sure how long I've been here."

"Drugs or booze, sir?"

"No, I sometimes - I kind of just sleepwalk."

"Sleepwalk? Right. Well, why don't you let me take you home? You have a place to stay?" the cop asked. Elgan was persuaded by her informality. He tried to shield the light to see her better.

"Uh, yeah, I live with my parents just around the corner. I could probably walk... I should be fine."

"You don't even have any shoes on." Her tact light flicked to his porcelain doll feet. "Come on. I won't tell them. Let's just get you home."

"I don't feel anything," he tried to say, but she grabbed him by the shoulder and directed him to the car.

"Just get in. I won't hurt you," she reassured him.

She guided him into the backseat, then got into the driver's side. He expected it to smell like puke or beer or smoke, but it smelt like a fading car freshener and old coffee.

She drove him for what seemed like an hour. He realised he didn't even give her his address.

"Where are we going?" he wondered as he looked out the window. They turned into a school's parking lot. "Where are we?"

"I just have to grab something from the back," she said and stepped out.

He heard her shuffling in the trunk. He wondered if he could just leave. He wondered if he should ask her if he could walk. He didn't want to antagonize her, but he felt wronged. Ashamed.

"You okay?" she prodded as she opened the driver side back-passenger door. She shuffled inside. Her hat, vest, and batman-style utility belt were off. Her shirt was buttoned open, and she held a black baton. "Are you scared of me? I'm not here to hurt you, love..." She shifted her body against him. "I get cold out here sometimes." She laid the edge of the black steel on his leg.

"I - uh - I don't think I can right now?" He tried to say, but he was sure it came out in unrecognisable stammers. "I just want to go, uh, home."

"Have you ever been with a woman? There're reports of men just like you going missing, you know. You're a handsome guy... I'm sure you have a mother that would miss you." She curled herself onto him. She began to open her blouse. He watched her button by button twist each one free. She lifted his hands and placed them on her breasts. "Have you ever felt these before?"

"I can't - I, uh..." he whispered pathetically.

She undid his jean's button and his zipper. She stretched them open with a tug. He watched her slide her hand onto his groin. His hands were frozen on her chest.

"Are you nervous?" She threw the baton to the side, as if expecting him to feel safer.

"No. No, I, uh..." he mumbled.

She moved off him and started shuffling off her dark cargo pants then her panties.

He was speechless. He was frozen. The shame swelled in his chest. He knew he should want it. He probably needed it, but his flaccid body shrank beneath her. He stressed about what she would do if he tried to force her off him. He didn't move. She suddenly leaned over him and shifted off his boxers. He looked as feelingless as he felt.

"Don't worry, honey... We can fix that." She leaned over him. He could see her put him in her mouth. He tried pulsating his entire being to his groin, but nothing happened. She continued to try, and he continued to let her. After countless minutes she looked up at him. "I know, honey... but maybe if you feel the real thing, that might help."

She re-wrapped herself onto him and shifted against him.

"I'm sorry... I - I can't feel anything. It's not -"

"What's wrong with you? You can't even fuck a woman?" she spat. She looked down at him with ugly eyes. She pushed off him and started redressing. He tried to speak, but he stumbled over his thoughts. "Of course you would be a weirdo... Why else would you be out in a park making noise. Fuck. Fuck me I'm stupid."

"I honestly... I wish–"

"Shut the hell up and get out. You can walk from here. You sick fuck. Get out. Get out!"

He tripped onto the cement as she rushed him out with his pants half-way up his legs. She got out in a flailing spin, dropped into the driver's seat, and sped off. He sat where he fell and watched the abyss of the night. He sat there with his pants at his knees knowing not a god damned person would believe him. He sat there and started to laugh.

6

It was him and the streetlights. Branches with swollen buds waving in slow motion. A black sky. Black earth. Sleeping porches. A fiction of life rolled out before him as Via Dolorosa in a nighttime haze. The truth served Elgan as faithfully as he served Christ. A world wallpapered in white lies to hide the mould. The willing blindness to marionette sex dolls driven by well-oiled machines. He wanted to understand, but it all led back to fear. Fear of what the world was making him become. Fear of trust. Fear of himself.

His barefooted steps were silent on the sidewalk. His trauma was silent in his head. He didn't believe it, let alone the idea that others would. Another story locked in a safe to give like a gift of his soul to someone who may one day listen and believe, but he knew no one would.

The leaves stopped waving at him. Day dimmed the darkness. He was disappointed in the realization that he had already reached his street.

He walked inside his house. The door hinges whined. He walked to the kitchen and poured a glass of water. He stood there and drank it. When he pulled the glass away from his mouth, his hands were shaking leaves. He clunked the glass onto the counter and looked out the window. He was staring right into his neighbour's washroom. Their light was on and the teenage girl who lived there was doing her own morning routine. He quickly snapped the curtains closed and walked to his room.

He was trapped in his head. The teenage girl in her window was the cop with her breasts spilling from her bra. The cop's face was split with laughter. She was a drooling pack animal. The boy with his head beneath Elgan's foot was a worm.

Elgan's cell phone suddenly rang, and he jumped.

"Hello," he answered.

"Is this Elgan Bluffs?" the woman on the other end asked.

"Yes."

"Hi Elgan, my name is Sophia. I'm with Grayton and Kapil. Did you submit an application to work as a Legal Assistant?" the woman said quickly. He missed her name. He tried to pull himself to the conversation.

"Ye - yes, that was me. Grayton and Kapil? Yes, I applied for that."

"Elgan, we'd like to invite you for an interview. Are you still interested in the position?"

"Uh, yes - Definitely." He circled on the spot trying to remember where he put his pen.

"That's great. Are you available this Thursday at Noon? It will be at the Grayton and Kapil office. We recently moved to Bay and Sheppardsville. Do you need the address? Your email on the resume, is it still the same?"

"Yes, it is."

"Okay, great, I'll email over the instructions to you. If you don't receive it by Thursday, please call this number back, okay?"

"Yes, okay. That's great." He ceased his panicked search for paper as he found his pen.

"Awesome. We're very excited to meet you.

See you Thursday," the woman said as the line went quiet.

He held the phone to his ear. He didn't blink. He didn't move. He stared at the crinkled yellowing pillow on his bed. He couldn't help but wonder at the oddity of life.

7

Elgan woke up to his alarm singing under his pillow. His phone showed ten-thirty. It was the seventeenth. He went to check the weather but decided instead to throw the phone back down. He closed his eyes for ten more minutes. His second alarm went off and he snoozed it. The snooze went off and he snoozed that. He determined to drag himself to the washroom by eleven-fifteen. He heard his alarm from his room go off as he finished dribbling his last remnants of piss into the toilet. He rushed quickly back to his room to shut it off. He opened his phone again and checked the news. The day's clickbait was an arm that was discovered by Lakefront Blvd. Below the suspected homicide article was *Thursday Market jitters shake the S&P.*

"Oh shit!" he swore with a flurry, throwing his

phone down and racing to his closet.

The days from the call for an interview seemed like a dream. Weird faces and sleeping silence. A drowsed bedridden stupor. He opened his email to confirm the address as he slipped on his nicest black pants, a white collared button up, and his favourite dark blue sweater.

Mid-day traffic snoozed past him as he dragged himself to the bus stop. The world seemed to naturally oppose his desperation. He checked his phone. It was eleven-thirty.

The bus stop was crowded with miscreants and tired-eyed women. Elgan wondered if the tired eyes and the miscreants were correlated: women exhausted of the fear of strangers' stares. Anxious in the unpredictability of each deviant because of the trauma induced by another's. Women who just wanted to get to work or find a breath of silence from an abusive world. Did they fear all men? Did they fear him? Maybe they were just tired because they had too many children and not enough time?

The bus soon arrived, and everyone shuffled on board except the miscreants, who stuck to the bus stop like roaches under a kitchen sink. It was eleven-thirty-five. He felt the time slipping away. He wanted to check his phone for interview tips, but he just watched himself in the blank screen.

After a cycle of stops, the bus arrived at Bay and Sheppardsville. It was eleven fifty-five. Most of the bus emptied. Elgan rushed through the casual crowd that spilled out of its centre and down a concrete alley. He found the building's door between store fronts and ran to the directory. He saw 'Grayton & Kapil - Second.' He bypassed the elevator and rushed in limping strides up the steps. The labyrinthine halls smelled of dust-filled vacuum bags. Open glass doors marked with businesses' and Doctors' names emitted whispering receptionist chatter. It was twelve-oh-two.

He found the Grayton and Kapil office and rushed inside and straight to the front desk. No one was there. He poked his head around the grey partitions and saw a woman's open handbag on the other side.

He waited a moment in pacing anxiety before he heard the clunking of heels.

"Oh, hello. How can I help you?" a woman inquired as she walked in and behind the desk. She held a red mug with steam lifting out of it.

"Hi - Hello. I'm Elgan Bluffs. I'm here for an interview," he said.

"Oh, didn't you... didn't you get the email?" She sat down and gave him a disgruntled look.

"I didn't see anything... One sec. One sec." He pulled out his phone and opened his email. Nothing was in the inbox. He opened his junk mail and saw it. "Cancelled? What do you mean? It's already been taken?"

"Yes. I'm very sorry, sir. We tried to warn you," she said. She took a sip of her coffee. "Oh, ouch. Still hot."

"Are you kidding me? I don't even get an interview? Are you kidding me? ARE. YOU. KIDDING. ME!?" He smashed everything off the desk's counter. Pens, paper, and a succulent shot against the wall. He heard the woman's screams through the clatter. "I, uh, I just need an interview. I just... I..."

The woman backed against the wall and her coffee spilled over her hand. She screamed and released the red mug. It shattered and sprayed the milky brown liquid across the floor. She was crying and swearing as she tried to desperately wipe the coffee off her skin.

"Get out!" the woman screamed. "Get out... Just get out. I'm calling the police."

"No - I - I didn't mean to... I... Oh shit." He watched her whimpering as she froze against the wall. He felt powerful. He felt like a man. He wanted her to shut up. She kept crying. He just wanted her to shut up. He tried to cover his ears, but the sound was trapped inside his head. "Shut up. Shut up. Shut up!" He kicked the desk. "Shut up!"

"Oh god..." she whimpered. "Daniel! Daniel!"

"Who's Daniel? Where is he?" Elgan wanted to calm her down. She wouldn't stop crying. "Why are you scared? It's okay. I'm not here to hurt you. It's okay. Just stop crying, okay?"

"What the hell..." a man said behind him. Elgan turned and saw the suited man. "Holy shit, man. What's going on in here? Sophia... Oh Christ. Dude what the hell?" The man suddenly rushed at Elgan, dropping the brown paper bag he had been holding.

He pulled Elgan by the neck of his shirt and slammed him against the wall. "What the hell is going on here?"

"I-it wasn't me. I'm just here... I, uh, I just was here for a job interview... I'm not sure what happened. She just won't stop crying. She won't stop crying," Elgan whimpered.

"Sophia, who the hell is this guy?" The man turned his head in search of the woman.

Elgan didn't resist, but he felt a beastly fury rising inside his stomach, aching with hunger.

"I'm nobody. Just a- just a guy..."

"Shut your goddamn mouth," the man spat. He was scared.

"Call the cops, Daniel... He's messed up... He's... Call the cops!" Sophia panicked. She was barely audible.

"Ha, women, eh?" Elgan released in a chortle through the man's arms that were compressed against his face. "I just wanted an interview. I think I'd be a good fit for the job."

"What the hell is wrong with you?" Daniel said wildly. The man looked nervous. Sweat dripped down his face like liquified balls of salt.

"What's it going to be then, eh? Why is everyone so shaky?" Elgan said from Daniel's chokehold. "I'm not anything bad. Even if I was, badness is something chosen. Does that still make me a man?" Elgan struggled against the man's tightening stranglehold. "I'm just trying to get over a slump. I'm just… I think there's been a misunderstanding. I don't want to hurt anyone."

"Man, you need goddamn Jesus Christ. Get out of here. Go get some help. If we see you around here again, we're calling the cops." Daniel tossed Elgan toward the door. "Get the fuck out of here, man. Calling the cops isn't worth it for scum like you…"

8

A wall of honking followed Elgan's stumble across the crosswalk. He felt disfigured beyond human likeness. What was he? Everyone pulled distasteful looks from him. They hated him. He hated himself most of all.

"Why..." he whispered. "Why?"

Shame hung from him like a forty-five on his old lifting belt. He didn't understand. He *didn't* understand. Each thread unravelled and split. Every step was haunted by the abuses of a cement reality. He was forgotten. A shell reanimated for the pummelling releases of society. He was forced to consume the honest flicker of a blink. The twitch of a lie. A physiognomical torture. He could see it all. He heard it in every word and silence. He hated them. Stupid and defiling. Abusive and manipulating. A stock of herd where the slaughterhouse was run by its own kind. Hogs selling hogs to other hogs for sides of ham to sell to the wolf. No one understood though. Everyone believed that they could become a wolf too, but a pig can never be a wolf because a pig is a pig.

"Jesus... Brother, are you alright?" a man said to him.

Elgan looked up. He had no memory of how he ended up on the ground in front of a coffee shop. The world spun in twisting dots.

"What are you doing out here like this? You'll get yourself abused and spat on by some self-righteous prick at this rate," the strange man said as he squatted beside Elgan.

Elgan looked up at him. The man looked like South American Jesus. Black hair like a samurai warrior. An ancient Mayan's face. His eyes were dark and sensitive, as if they felt the pain of humanity.

"Who are you?" Elgan whispered.

"I'm just a guy walking by," the man said. "What happened, man? You don't look good. A guy like you wearin' clothes like that shouldn't be laying out here on the street."

"I'm lost..." Elgan mumbled. "I'm lost, but I got nowhere to go." He pushed himself back against the wall behind him. "I can feel the concrete walls closing in around me. I can feel the hate and the rage. I can feel everything in my head like a pulsing cold sore, but I can't *feel* it! I can't feel my fingertips or my toes. Not the pain nor the pleasure. How do I know – how do I know what is right? How do I know what I need? I can't feel it... I can't feel anything!"

"Take a breath, man. Take a breath." The man didn't take his eyes off Elgan's. Elgan found himself analysing the man's yellowed teeth and earthy smell. Would Jesus Christ be so flawed? "This won't be the last thing to hurt you, man. This probably won't be the last time you find yourself here, but next time when you do, just remember to breathe. It'll be easier next time now that you've been here, that's for sure. You'll see soon too... You'll have a new intuition for it. You'll see the strange threads of strangers now. Not like some sci-fi bullshit, but you'll see the reality. Most people never get here, you know. They stay trapped in their heads like the loyal mutts they are, but now you're here." Elgan stared wide-eyed at the man as he went on: "all of the faces, the love, the fear... the destitution, you'll feel every inch of it. It's the burden of truth. Now *you* have to decide what to do with it, and only your heart can tell you that. And buddy, don't think this is me telling you I have any idea what the hell I'm doing. The truth is, I don't think anyone really does. Just stay away from the drugs, man. I've had to spray naloxone into two friends, and despite giving them life again, they hated me as much as they hated themselves. I still bring sandwiches to my old buddy who lost sight in an eye from being beaten over a bad angel dust deal. Here. Take this, man, and know that there are others. Take it..."

"Other what?" Elgan pressed, reaching for the oat bar the man handed him.

"Humans. Those unpolarized by a society rotating around them like opposing magnets. Those who see the truth. Who live with their dreams instead of just sleep with them. Anyway, I would honestly stay and chat, but my missus can get a little loopy if I'm gone too long," the man chuckled as he stood from his squat. "The pain never goes away; you just have to find something that makes managing it worthwhile. Seek forgiveness for yourself. I ain't no lordly man, but maybe you could find some solace in the Bible?

There's also a hospital just a few blocks from here... Queen's Memorial, there's a really good program, man. It could change your life." The man smiled down at Elgan. "And remember to breathe. Shit, I better find my woman before she finds me. She'll be giving me the googly eyes if I'm not careful."

"Thank you," Elgan said, but it didn't feel like enough.

The man threw a wave as he walked away. He wore blue jeans and was wide shouldered. He was short, but sturdy. He walked with the carelessness of a free soul.

Elgan opened the oat bar and ate it. He tried to think beyond the sensation of feeling like a rat nibbling its scavenged goods in the corner, but it was pointless. He would never be a bear again, only a rat.

9

The overwhelming stench of a bubbling deep fryer made Elgan's stomach gassy as he helped his mom set the table for dinner. Forks on the right on top of the napkin, spoons on the left with the knife. Cup on the right above the fork, glass, not plastic. He filled the three glasses with water then sat at his normal spot.

"How'd the interview go, honey?" his mom asked. She placed a bowl of oily French fries in the middle of the table and returned to prepping the rest of the dinner.

"Umm, it went good, I hope. They seemed impressed." He didn't know why it was so easy to lie to her.

"That's really great. Do you know when they'll let you know?"

"Let me know what?" He looked down at his

empty plate. He wasn't interested in talking to any-one.

"If you got it or not."

"Oh. Yeah. They said they'd let me know within two weeks or something like that."

"Great. Great. Make sure you write down a reminder to give them a call if they don't call you by then," she said with a smile as she brought over a pot of green beans.

"Yeah, that's a good idea," he said.

They shared a look down the hall as the front door opened and shut. Elgan's dad shuffled in. He slipped off his driving runners.

"Hey hun, I just made the basics tonight," his mom said, walking over and giving his dad a welcoming peck.

"Sounds good. I just have to get changed," his dad said. "How'd the interview go, bud?"

"Good." Elgan knew there was no satisfaction in the duty his dad fulfilled in speaking to him. He was unsure if he should say more or not. "I, uh, I can let you know later, if you like?"

"Yeah, sure. Sounds good." His dad walked past

them toward the bathroom.

When his dad came back with pyjamas on, they ate. They ate quietly. The sound of his dad's squishing chews drove him insane, but he held it in without a flinch.

"You hear about the mugging? Just up the road by the store," his mom said through a swallowed mouthful. "It's getting bad around here."

"Damned gang bangers are bringing their problems further and further east. You can't even walk up the street without being accosted by some homeless or some punks," his dad complained. Elgan wondered if gang bangers haunted his dad's sleep. "These bullshit policies in this country are running us into the dirt. You can't even feel safe in your own God damned home. Conservatives didn't do jack when they were elected, and now we got socialist Orange Party donkeys driving prices up and increasing disparity for those just looking to survive. Now we got the kids of those people who have no choice but to find an income, sacrificing their own children's needs. Nobody seems to want to be responsible for their own offspring these days. It's all bullshit, I tell ye."

"Did they catch who did it?" Elgan asked, ignoring his dad's tangent.

"No, that's the scary part. I hope they bring it up on the news tonight. I couldn't find anything online." his mom gossiped. "Suzana said that when she was walking Michelle, she saw a group of boys rough housing at the park. She said she couldn't even walk into it because the boys were all over the place and yelling and swearing. She said she could smell their weed. I don't know... I think we should think about maybe moving. Especially with this and those stories about people going missing downtown."

"Ash, come on. Where would we go? This isn't a good time for me. I don't think I can jump into anything big right now-"

"I know. I was just saying. I'm sorry my safety isn't worth your time, your majesty," his mom interrupted.

"Oh, calm down, Ashley. I'm just saying we should talk about it some other time." His mom shook her head and went on eating. "Elgan getting out there though and going for a job. Good job, bud. A man ain't a man if he ain't working."

After dinner Elgan returned to his room. The white ceiling was a preferred landscape for his mind. A flat white like a pressed doctor's jacket. He wanted to sleep. He wanted to close his eyes and wake up with the energy of some form of living. Maybe he would wake up as the man his father seemed to imagine he was.

He looked at his phone and opened his last conversation with Raleigh. The two-year-old date stamp was strangely comforting. He stared at her picture. He tried to hate her. It was so easy to hate the rest of the world, to hate himself, to despise her friends, to lie to his family, but he felt a curse of need when he saw her rounded eyes, like almonds carved out of aged porcelain.

He turned his head to the sprawled weights. He dragged himself off the bed and walked over to them. He picked up the thirty-five. He understood the gravity that pulled it down, but he felt nothing. He curled it. He did thirty reps, put it down and started push-ups. The motions lacked purpose. He got bored and sat beside his bed. There was no pump nor pain. His eyes were on the back of his computer chair, but his mind was tripping through left open compart-ments of anxiety. Raleigh's face seemed to creep out of each one.

Was he obsessed? Two years of silence in the palm of his hand. He felt like a stalking predator. Maybe she was thinking about him too? The world seemed smaller with her in it. He whipped his phone at his desk and hung his head to the floor. He wondered if he was supposed to report these delusions to a doctor.

The house's silence crept into his mind. Raleigh's eyes penetrated deeper. He tried to strangle his vision with his eyelids, but she watched him from every angle. She was always watching him.

He moved to his hands and knees and crawled over to his phone on the floor. He checked his notifications. Nothing.

He remembered that she used to tell him that letters were the key to her heart. How come nobody ever asked what the key to his heart was? He felt painfully lonely. Lonely to his gut. A feeling of old coffee congealing inside him. He wanted to puke, but he found himself rushing to the bathroom to shit instead. Another feelingless release.

He stared at the wall thoughtlessly as he tried to breathe through his diarrhoean mess. Its release relieved none of the anxiety.

He wiped and flushed and washed his hands. He splashed water onto his head and looked at himself in the mirror. The lighting gave him a jaundiced complexion. He wanted to talk to himself to see what he looked like talking. He just stared. Sunken amber eyes, big ears, wispy hair. Unfelt drops dripping off his chin.

He left the washroom and laid down in his bed. It was raining again. He watched as individual droplets caught each other, danced in a pool, then split away. Sometimes the drops met and trailed off as one. He turned away to avoid the metaphor.

He lay there in his head. Eyes with brunette blurs watched him. He couldn't escape their fiendish concern. Why did he need what he couldn't have?

"Fuck! Fuck. Fuck. Fuuuuuck," he repeated.

He needed to go see her. He needed to get her back. He craved to see her again. She would understand. He wasn't stalking her. He *loved* her. If the aching pain in his chest wasn't love, he might as well be dead. Brown eyes, brown hair, with a smile that twisted his soul. He put his head into the palm of his hands and pulled at his hair. He couldn't even feel it. He couldn't feel anything but emotional angina. He *needed* her. The fantasy of her haunted him. He needed to run. He had to see her.

He got up in a spin and threw on his pants and an Atreyu shirt. He rushed past his mom, who was working late at the table. She didn't even look up. The News from the living room spoke of another missing soul, lost to the city's serrated edge. He slipped on his shoes and stealthily raced outside.

He had to see her.

10

Rain left the pavement black. Grey clouds smogged the sky. Elgan ran with desperate depravity. The wind's moist residue were sensationless kisses on his face.

He found Raleigh's street and stopped at the corner. The breeze tugged his clothing. The sidewalk seemed to stretch onward as if there was an approaching Nazgûl. His hands were shaking uncontrollably. His thoughts begged him to keep going. He urged his phantom legs onward to drown the noise in his head.

The suburban houses were almost completely identical. Trees on the boulevard, sidewalk separating the boulevard from a grass yard, a four-patio stone square off a cracking-greyed driveway, a front door, and a bay window with a half-assed garden muddied below it. Some houses had tricycles and kids' toys; another had a dark red tree as tall as his shoulders.

Her house was at the bend in the road. Forest green, with a monastery door. Droplets fell from her eaves like World Trade Center divers. He stared at her bay window in a daze of clouded fear. The curtains were open, and the light of a dining room let him see right through. They were sitting around their table eating dinner. He could see the dark brown hair spilling down her back. Her dad on the left end of the table, her mom on the right. Her mom talked animatedly. Raleigh dropped something and she leaned down. Elgan could see her brother who looked up from his plate and saw him.

"Shit!" Elgan spat between his teeth. He ducked down and ran to the side of the neighbour's house. "Shit."

He was a freakshow. His heart was racing somewhere beneath his ribs. Did other people do this? Something had to be wrong with him. He was a stalker. This is what a stalker was.

He poked out from between the cedar bushes he had tucked himself into and continued to watch

Raleigh's house. No one came outside. He statued there trapped in watchful fear.

Day time slipped away with coattails of dark blue. Droplets fell from the branches above him. Wet leaves licked at his arms. His body convulsed in an unfelt shiver. He shuffled backwards out of the hedge. Water sprayed from the wheels of a passing car.

Saudade haunted Elgan. A craving so deep he was blind. Blind and deaf. Curses on an already cursed corpse. Rotting bones of a dug-up child of Akhenaten. Desiderium accretion swelling his amygdala.

"What the Christ am I doing?" he whispered to himself. He couldn't feel a damned thing and yet here he was, driven by the napalm in his head.

He stumbled to the sidewalk. He somehow unearthed the resolve in himself to go back to his bed, but the sound of an opening door behind him persuaded him to look.

There she was. It was *her*. Just as she was in his dreams and his memories. He felt disarmed. Was she supposed to see him? He wanted to run, but he *wanted* her to see him. He could hear her calling good-bye to her parents. Her dark hair was like waves of rolling fondue. She was smiling. She wore slim blue jeans and a black sweater. She tucked her hands into her pockets and shrugged with the energy of joviality. They were all laughing. He could see her smile. She turned and her eyes caught him. He stopped breathing.

"Oh, uh," he stumbled backward. He couldn't say anything else.

"Elgan? What are you doing here?" Her face cracked like a splitting cold sore. She was a hideous retch. He melted into the damp cement. A toy soldier caught in a ray of sunlight. She shook her head in confusion. He couldn't move! Her medusan stare crippled him. "Elgan?"

"I-I, uh, I'm sorry. I didn't know you still lived here. I was just... uh," he stuttered. The words stuck to his tongue as masticated toffee. "I was just walking by."

He could see her mom staring at him worriedly from their front step. He couldn't summon the courage to look back at Raleigh. He was almost completely a pool puddled with the rain into the sidewalk. They would have to peel him off to move him once he dried up.

Raleigh's mom looked with knowing concern at Raleigh, who he was physically unable to see anymore. He heard Raleigh say, "okay..." Then he heard the starter of a car. He smelt its exhaust. He drank it into his lungs like a dehydrated wildebeest. He heard the car's suspension as it dropped in a wild reversal from the driveway to the road. There was a light squeal as the car peeled away. She was gone. How long had he been standing there?

He saw her mom look from side to side then go back inside. He saw the curtains slightly drawn at the front window, a crack of accusing shame in an otherwise pristine home. He finally caught his breath as the wind shoved him. Each recovery breath that bellowed out of his nostrils brought him back to standing balance. He was normal. He was just walking by. He was normal. It was all a complete coincidence.

11

It was late by the time Elgan got home. The world had been a timeless blur. He struggled to believe anything was real. It all had seemed a delusional trial he concocted and failed with every attempt to understand. People popped up in strange moments of life, but they were never real. He didn't seem real. He was a side-character in a distorted film reel.

His mom was still working at the table. Her hair-bun drooped to her ear. Her black-bagged eyes were unblinking. The click of her fingers on the keyboard converted the house into a hospital reception. He was the delusional patient wandering the halls.

He pissed, brushed his teeth obsessively, then caved into his bed like the proper dependant he was. He could hear the keyboard clicking through his door. Spiders tap dancing on roller skates.

He closed his eyes, but the clicking was worse than a room full of clocks.

Humanity bled out of his pores as he laid there in the darkness. It drowned him: a tentacled monster latching its tendrils onto its prey and pulling it into the black depths. A seaman's nightmare. Did Jesus ever experience unrequited physical desire? Was Jesus celibate? Was he involuntarily celibate?

Raleigh's horrified face mocked Elgan as he struggled with the urges of his own desires.

His loneliness grew desperate.

He was a ghost, floating as a dream in a cloud. Gusted away in an unexpected rush of air. He floated, touched the ground and bounced as if he was jumping on the surface of the moon. There was no one around. There was only the absence of feeling. He was a leaf. He lacked flight, but the natural state of life carried him. He got suddenly caught in a twist of deep brown. Chocolate brown. Roots coming up of the earth, entangling him. The darkness consumed him. He was crying.

A knock vibrated through his head.

"You still up, dude?" his dad asked through the

bedroom door.

Elgan shot up.

"Yeah – yeah, I'm awake. Everything okay?" he asked dazedly.

"We're going out for a bit. A pump went down on site and mum's coming with me for the drive. Just wanted to give you a heads up."

"Okay, thanks."

Elgan's head hit the pillow. He listened to see if he could hear them pull away, but there was nothing.

He stepped out of the room and tiptoed down the hall after waiting as long as his body was willing. He skulked. He was a patient whose room was accidentally left unlocked. He peeked stealthily out the side window. They were gone. The naked loneliness crept up his spine. He checked his parent's room. He checked the washroom. They were gone.

He went into their room and started looking through their closet. He fingered the frills of an old leather jacket. He opened a tucked box and found it filled with perfumes. He opened another box and found a blue dildo, lubricant, and some porn magazines. He looked through them carelessly and put the box aside. He pulled out a hard case from between some junk and opened it. A gun was inside. A black metal pistol. It was his dad's dildo. It had a lock over its trigger. He investigated the corners of the box. There was nothing else. There was another box tucked underneath a folded sheet. He twisted it open. A box of bullets and a key were inside. He wasn't surprised at his dad's mental viscosity. He put the key in the trigger lock and peeled it off.

He put the box of bullets and the gun on the bed and attempted to return the emptied closet back to its original state. The sweat in his eyes told him he wasn't going fast enough. He shoved the final box in and dragged the hanging clothes back into place, grabbed the black deadweight and bullets, and escaped back to his room.

He shut and locked his door then sat on his bed. He twisted the crafted, steel ebony in his hands. Dark and deathly. A single shot could kill a person. A single shot could ruin them. Like a car accident in the palm of your hand. One bullet and a barrel flash. How much blood would really come out? Did it release in a spray? Every movie seemed to show it differently, as if no one really knew. The only people who seemed to know never wanted to put it into words. Maybe those people were afraid to show how easy it really was.

He slid ten bullets into the gun's clip. Each one clicking into place as he pushed it down. He slid the magazine inside. The final click was erotic. He tried to tuck it into his pants, but he couldn't get it to feel secure. He ran to the kitchen and grabbed his mom's laptop bag and placed it inside. The daze of life followed him out the door.

It seemed too obvious to go straight back to Raleigh's parents, but he had to do it: he had to know if she was still real.

He passed through the empty park. The crystal tipped grass darkened his shoes. The landscape moved by on a conveyor. There was a person on a bench up ahead who was spot-lighted by a park light. They floated like a dream. He was suddenly afraid to stare. What if they knew he was analysing them? He watched them from his peripherals. He judged them. He consumed people then dumped them, knowing they'd never satisfy his need. He drained them like a vampire and left their corpses to be pecked by carrion. He didn't need fangs to tap into a person's soul and leave it wanting, weeping, and weak. He wasn't a moral man. He was a sycophant, a serpent, a slave. A slave to himself. He was a spinning top.

"Hi," the person from the bench said. It was a woman. He was next to her, standing there, watching her. She had a strange face.

"Hi... I, uh, I'm just walking through," he said.

"Your ensemble is very nice." She looked him up and down with a child's smile, but a woman's eyes.

"Uh..." He looked down at his black pants and Atreyu shirt. "Thanks?"

"Who did your hair?"

"I did it myself."

"How long did it take you? It's very nice."

"I don't know. I just woke up like this."

"I'm Daniella. D for deadly. A for ambitious." She started to laugh. He had the feeling that she was making fun of him, but he doubted himself.

"Um, my name's Elgan."

"That's a nice name. I live at Central Street. I like coming here to see the birds. See. See that one.

That's a warbler. That's a warbler right there. Isn't that nice? A nice warbler. What would you name him? I'd name him Snoopy."

"Oh, I don't know."

"Snoopy looks hungry. Do you have any snacks for him? Snoopy looks like such a good boy. You know it is a boy, right?"

"I'm not sure. I don't know anything about birds."

"It's got those red streaks on its chest. See the red streaks? I saw it on TVO. Red streaks is for a boy. I'm not a boy. I'm a girl. I'm twenty-three. Are you twenty-three? You have nice eyes. They match your ensemble. Do you have a dog?"

"A dog? I'm not sure I follow."

"Baby, let me follow you down! Baby, let me follow you down! I do anything if you just just come home, just come home, with you!" she belted. Her voice cracked and she snorted and shook with the boisterousness of a free child. "That's my pa's song. He sang it to my mumma. You know pa and mumma? Old fashioned twists. Old fashioned toes." Elgan sat down beside her. He didn't know what he was looking for, but her innocence calmed his fight or flight. "You can call me Dani. My class calls me Dani-O. People in my old school called me Down Dani-O. Down Dani-O, don't drink the drainoooo."

"Where did you go to school?" He didn't know what else to say. She seemed content just speaking on her own behalf. He pitied her *and* envied her.

"Do you make your own bed?" she asked.

"Uh, yeah. You didn't answer my question though. I'm wondering what school you went to?"

"I went to a school with kids, boys, men, and teachers. Mr. Harlish was a wise handler, they told me. I just liked the library corners. It's really something special where two bookcases meet. Something special in the gap where no bookishness is. I saw light there. Mr. Harlish showed himself to me there as I watched the light. He was a wise handler. One on one for a child of intellectual needs, while they tried to plant intellectual seeds they say would blossom into me. I blossomed into me. I don't need no seeds. I didn't need seeds. Baby! Let me foll-llow you down!"

Elgan stood up slowly, but she put her big hand

on his laptop bag. She pinched the pistol as if she knew it was there the whole time. He pushed her hand away more aggressively than he intended.

"Please! Sorry… just, you shouldn't touch other people's things," he snapped.

She started to moan and squeal in an odd succession. She spat on the ground and turned her smiling face up to his. She looked confused and hurt despite her crooked teeth pressed together in a visible grin.

"You shouldn't shout at people. You shouldn't shout at people you don't know. My mumma would say, 'don't you talk like that to my girl. Mister, don't you talk like that. She's special. She's a special girl. You blind?' I used to go to school with a blind boy. Isaiah, the boy with silent eyes. I wish I had silent eyes. I could watch the thoughts in my head like a merry-go swinging to and fro. To-n-fro, to-n-fro. Swing like a merry-go."

She grabbed Elgan's hand. If she was a normal woman, he would have thought it was a sexual flirtation, but he felt shame instead. Shame like a man taking advantage of a child whose innocence blinds them. He pulled away quickly but smiled back at her. She seemed unphased and kept her jack-o-lantern grin on him as if the interaction never occurred.

"Is it okay if I just sit here and watch the birds with you, and then I'll have to be on my way?" he asked.

"Yes. I think that - that would be nice."

It was more awkward than her singing. Her breathing was heavy and open mouthed. He could see her twiddling and twitching, and yet he couldn't walk away. Was he afraid? He didn't understand what was holding him there. He started to laugh. Afraid! He looked over at her. She was watching the edge of the darkness. She looked over at him, suddenly realizing his laughter. He was shaking and struggled to keep his eyes on her. Afraid!

"Is it me? Am I funny? Is it me?" She grew suddenly manic.

"No - no, not you. I'm not laughing at you. I just - I just think..."

The laughter burst out of him like a main break. It seeped from him. He emptied all over the ground and into the air. The bench floated away in a daze. The woman was a blur of squealing reciprocation as he fell to the ground.

"You're funny. You're really funny." She stared over him and laughed spittle at him. Her twisted teeth were spread in an echoing expulsion of noise. Cracked glass-eyed face like a rock crushed Piggy.

She tried to help him up by pulling on his bag, but the shoulder strap snapped. She stumbled backward into the bench with the bag clutched to her chest.

"I-I-I-I was just trying to help. I was just trying to help you." She started to cry.

She spontaneously reached into the bag and pulled out the gun. Her eyes were an inflated black.

"It's okay... You can give me that." Elgan reached out his hand as gently as he could manage. Her mouth breathing was animalistic. The unconscious fear became a reality.

"Down Dani-O, don't drink the draino. Down Dani-oooo." She stood up. The gun dangled stupidly in her loose grip. She leaned forward with the gun aimed at his chest. "D for deadly. A for ambitious. Are you going to hurt me? Are you going to hurt me, mister?"

"No. Why - why would I do that? Dani, please give me the gun?"

"Did you hurt people before?"

"Dani...give me the gun."

"Did you hurt any people?" She stepped closer. She was vibrating.

"No. No, I don't hurt people. I haven't hurt anyone... I'm just a weak idiot."

"Then you're going to hurt yourself? Mr. Elgan handsome, you said you don't hurt people. Not like me. I hurt people. N for... N for..." He slapped her wrist and tried to wrestle the gun from her, but her manic desperation disoriented him, and he spun in a mess back to the ground. She stepped over him and pointed the gun down at his stomach. He watched her finger pressing against the trigger, but nothing happened. She just breathed in sprays of ragged breath. Her goggle-glasses were at the edge of her nose. "N for naughty. Naughty naughty Dani. She's wearing white panties." She laughed, dropped the gun, and fell back on the bench. She fell into hysterics.

Elgan scooped up the gun in a whiplash. He

turned to leave but she grabbed his wrist again. "I tried to do it. I tried to do it, but it wouldn't work."

She whipped his hand down and stumbled away. She was gone. He noticed his hand was shaking. He tucked the gun back into the bag and looked around. Her sudden abandonment made the world feel like an empty stage. He saw only the absence of people. A true loneliness. The expectation of human acknowledgement had forsaken him. He felt as if he had aged five years in fifteen minutes. He was a feelingless ghost. A walking shadow. A corpse of chaotic energy drawing out the fear of people's hearts. A world of windowless walls slowly closing him in, locking him inside the last refuge of his self. The only refuge. Despite all the fear and the anxiety, he still felt nothing. He wished she had been able to do it. At best he would've finally been able to put the demons to sleep. At worst...

His body shuddered through his next breath.

Weakness could not become him. Weakness would not become him, he repeated to himself. His phantom body obeyed and carried him onward toward Raleigh's parent's house.

12

The sky was crowded by heavy, black clouds, tinted by an edging azure. Dawn crept in as an adulterous husband. Elgan watched Raleigh's house from the store parking lot across the street. A light was on in her upstairs window. He tried to remember what room it could be by the last time he was there and calculated that it was probably the washroom. Her car was back in the driveway.

A drop of rain slapped the ground. A barrage followed. He wanted to scream. The rain rolled off him in unfelt streams. An external numbness inflated the chemical ache that broiled inside the cavity of his chest. He felt the laptop bag to remind himself why he was there. He stood up and walked into the spotlight of the parking lot light. He stopped and haunted her house with his mind. He imagined climbing the wood fence into her back yard and slipping through the sliding glass door they always had left unlocked. He'd take off his shoes. The gun would be in his hands. He'd find her mom and dad in their own chairs watching TV. He'd put them at peace first. Their blood would run along the crevice of the deep brown hardwood in sync with the rain that dripped down the bay window.

His eyes shot open. There was nothing left of his soul but the remnants broken and dusty in his gut. Snapped drywall in a condemned hovel.

A random car's yellow lights hit the window of every home it splashed passed.

"Fuck! Fu-uck..." The world emptied itself on top of him and he collapsed to the pavement.

The gun's shaking barrel was all he could picture. He curled closer into himself. He was the skin that was shed. A better version of him floated away from the world, as he cracked and snapped. The rain danced off its own puddles, as he watched at eye level.

A memory of the hospital's IV drip bubbled into his thoughts. Raleigh stood beside it as he stared at the refraction of fluorescent off the bag. She had kept on her jacket. Her eyes revealed the disgust in her heart. Had they always been that way or was it the circumstance of the memory? She had stared down at him with porcelain doll eyes without saying a word. Not a word, a sound, or twinge of empathy. When her lips had finally parted, she had spoken to him the last words he would hear from her for more than two years: "who will you be if you don't die in here?"

Raleigh was suddenly nothing. The obsession melted away. He rolled onto his back and let the rain baptise his face. He started to laugh. He always imagined madness to come as a single moment, but he suddenly realized that each moment in his control was a respite from the daunting beast that sheltered in place of his soul.

He unzipped his mom's sopping laptop bag and pulled out the pistol. He cocked it and put the barrel against his head. He couldn't stop laughing. He really didn't understand how people could do it. He didn't understand why anybody would. Even with nothing left, there was still the spontaneity of hope, wasn't there? A hope curled inside, sleeping, dreaming of waking. What hope had he had when she left him that day? A paraplegic slug wrapped in the linen cocoon of what he thought would be his forever home. And yet here he was, a phantom walking with the power of painlessness. Would he eventually feel the entropy and decay of his risen corpse or would death for him be another sensationless sleep?

He put the gun back in the bag, pulled himself up, and looked at the window one last time. He didn't have his phone or any money, so he followed the sidewalk toward downtown, past strip malls and beer stores, through the rain scattered dark blue of a new morning until he found Queen's Memorial hospital. It glowed ghostly white.

He saw a dumpster tucked into a nearby apartment alley. The rain splashed off its closed lid. He rushed over to it and leaned against it to puke. The splatters of reddish orange were masked by the downpour. He washed his face in a puddle then tossed the laptop bag into the dumpster bin.

The gaunt halls called to him, and he heeded their demands. A red sliver of the rising sun was reflected in the glass windows of the hospital's vestibule.

13

Elgan felt like he'd gone a long way from the bodybuilder that was rolled under the watchful white, fluorescent that seemed to line the ceiling of every hospital hallway. His cold shadow was paraded through the labyrinth. The walls expanded and closed in like a cycling organ. The woman helping him was talking, but he didn't hear a word. He didn't even know if she worked there.

She left him at the door of the ward. It was a heavy-duty double door with two glazed windows but no handles. A buzzer was on an adjoining wall. He pressed it and it buzzed lightly.

"How can we help you?" an overly loud voice answered with a clicking sound.

He leaned into the small speaker and said, "uh, self-admission."

The double doors clicked, and the speaker buzzed. The doors swung open with the automaticity of a store greeter. The women at the reception desk eyed him with wary smiles.

He filled in paperwork, was given a tour, and provided a space. He had tinnitus. His stomach twirled. He was sitting on a bed in a room crossed between a dentist's office and a motel. The other bed across the room was unmade. The room was cold.

He got up and went into the hall. It was cozy. A soft blue. Welcoming chairs were paired and tucked into cubbies with window lookouts. There was a reading room. There was a coffee room. There were booths for calling out. He felt safer here than at his local park. The open windows brought in the cool breezes of the new morning. There was one man sitting at a window drawing, but no one else that he heard or saw.

When he found the end of the ward at the reception desk, he smiled and turned back. He sat down at a chair in the reading room and fell into the depths of his own thoughts. It was a muddied cesspool, but he saw himself as he was: a tired man.

Man... He hadn't considered that word for himself in years. Could a cripple be a man? What does a soldier become after he loses both legs? Could he possibly be the same man?

"Hi," said a voice that startled him.

"Uh, hi," he said quickly, expecting a nurse.

"How are you?" the woman asked.

Her brown eyes locked him in place, but somehow his mouth released the right words, "just great."

She laughed. He laughed. They were both laughing. Why was he laughing? They were both still laughing. He must've actually looked like an insane person, but her laugh seemed so amazing and fresh that it pulled him along. They both locked eyes again.

"So awkward..." she said. Her face was red, and she looked around.

He'd never seen anyone like her. An immovable force. Her eyes suffocated him. They consumed him. Was he breathing? He had to breathe. He pulled his eyes away and looked around.

"I'm Elgan."

"I'm Lily."

"Lily?"

"It's Ukrainian."

"You're Ukrainian?"

"No, I'm... I don't really know what I am. Caucasian."

"You're adopted or something?"

"Yes. You know it was a joke, right? I'm not actually Ukrainian."

He stared at her. The silence wasn't as horrible as he would have expected. She watched him. She was still smiling.

"Are you okay?" he asked.

"Oh - I - I was just saying hello. Not too many people seem to wake up this early in here."

"How long have you been in here?"

"Oh, just three or four nights."

"Ah, you just sound like you've been here a while," he said.

"What does that mean?" She looked appalled.

"I just mean like you sound like you know the place."

"Well maybe I just pay attention a little more than most?"

"Do you like it here?"

"It serves its purpose."

"You know, you're the one who initiated this. If you're not enjoying my company, you can leave at any time."

"Why do you think I'm not enjoying your company?" she asked.

The genuine curiosity that cupped her chin sent alarms through his chest. He needed to be calm. Her dark hair was tied into a ponytail. He tried not to look anywhere else than her but her eyes, but they sliced into him. She pulled away as he did. Did she see the sheen of nervous sweats on his face?

He adjusted himself. "I just... I haven't had a proper conversation with anyone in a long time. It feels... foreign."

"Oh," is all she said. She looked at him thoughtfully then looked away.

"*Are* you enjoying *my* company?" he asked.

She looked at him and smiled. "Why are you here?"

"I think I'm... I don't know. I'm scared. I feel weak. I feel wilted. I'm a cripple dragging my feelingless body around. I'm stuck in this mask that I didn't choose. I try to rip it off. I try to put a new one on, a new face... but everyone sees a dilapidated child, as if each new mask is cracked and revealing the weak boy underneath. I'm confined in a spiral of disapproving looks and emasculating aggressions. I feel trapped."

"Do you feel trapped right now?"

"No... No - I-"

"Maybe you just need someone to talk to?" she suggested. "Have you tried any medication?"

"Medication? Like what, antidepressants or something?"

"Sure. There's lots of help you can get."

"Well, is it working for you?" he asked sarcastically.

"I guess that really depends on if you're real or not," she said with a smirk.

"I'm struggling to tell if you're joking."

"Well, I'm always joking and always serious."

He burst out laughing and ran his hands through his hair.

"What are you talking about? Has anyone ever told you that you're really funny?"

She looked away then sat down in a chair across from him. She pulled her legs to her chest and wrapped her arms around them. She watched him over her knees.

"Are you afraid of yourself?" she asked. The soul in her eyes drew him in.

"I don't know... I might be. I'm afraid of what I am now, I guess. I wasn't always like... this." he said.

"Oh yeah? What were you like before?"

"I felt taller. Confident. I smiled more. I worried less. I had power over myself. I was stronger and healthier. I drove and worked and had friends and saw women. I was a man."

"A man?"

"I... I don't know what I am."

"You look like a man. You're honest like a man. I think maybe you worry too much about it."

"Well, that's why I'm here."

"Right," she said softly.

"You don't believe me?"

"I think you need to spend some time looking for who you are. You don't seem to know yourself."

He felt as if she saw right through him and yet

didn't see him at all. "Maybe *you* don't know yourself," he shot back.

"I guess that's why I'm here," she snapped in return. "And not because of my craving to commit serial murder."

"Hey, how are you two doing?" a nurse asked as she walked into the room with an empty cup.

The nurse slipped her cup into the coffee maker, put a pod in, and closed it. The waft and sound of brewing lessened the awkwardness of the silence. Lily was looking away. He couldn't help but watch her. She looked back at him. He felt trapped again.

"Well, I should go. It was nice meeting you," Lily waved. She stood up and lingered a glance on him. "Bye."

She was gone. Did he even watch her go? She just vanished in a flicker of a moment.

The coffee maker spewed its contents. The aroma was more chemical than coffee. The nurse left the room. The room stank like an unkempt café.

14

I *give so much, hoping... hoping that one day someone will give it all back in return*, Elgan thought, as a blurred memory of her face mystified his mind. Lily. He would never forget her eyes.

The room spun. He wanted to get up, but his numbed limbs were extra heavy. He was no more than a swollen drunk. The thought of her sat on his chest. The mental weight was immovable. The room swirled and swirled, and he lay there like the tip of a spinning top.

Blue watched him through a crack in the closed curtains. He had slept for hours. He couldn't tell what had been a dream and what had been real. Maybe it all had been real or none of it? Maybe *she* wasn't even real.

He laid there, lost in his head. Lost in the

imagination of a life with a dream woman who saw into his soul. Maybe it was a delusion? Was he sick? Is that why he admitted himself? The world seemed closer. Closing in.

There was a knock on the door. He wanted to get up, but he couldn't. They knocked again, then it stopped. He closed his eyes for a second and opened them to a room fully lit by daylight. The curtains were opened. The room was more white than blue. He could move. He got up and went piss. He even had the energy to lift the seat.

The hall smelt like porridge, coffee, and isopropyl alcohol. He walked past a man reading a magazine in a window cubby and went into the reading room. It was busier than the morning. A man paced by the sink. He was counting something on his fingers. A boy no older than nineteen sat alone at a table and slowly spooned his food. A young woman sat at another table with an older lady, and they were both reading different novels. Any internal spectres of *One Flew Over the Cuckoo's Nest* were gone. He felt safe.

He spent three days and two nights living in a

strange world of comfortable derealization. His mind craved a sign of Lily, but he never saw her for the rest of stay.

15

Elgan satisfied the discharge requirements by Sunday afternoon. He had stayed only for a chance to see her again, but he embraced his monarch reprogramming with the hopes that she would see his improvement and emerged from the hospital a dilapidated butterfly. He took a cab home. His parents didn't even seem to notice that he had been gone. His mom was still at the table working, despite it being Sunday. His dad looked at him with a quizzical expression and kept on eating his toast. He went to his room and locked the door. He was soaked in sweat. He stripped and stood in front of the mirror. Hairy legs, a protruding tummy, arms like loosened noodles. He swayed and tried to flex his torso. He always ended up back in front of his virtual self, watching as a stranger, expecting a different result. He pulled his clothes back on and sat at the edge of his bed. He wished he had kept the gun.

When he found the desire to go grab some food, his parents were gone.

He made a peanut butter and jelly sandwich, grabbed some water and sat at his computer. He looked up Lily using every search engine he could think of. She was living rent-free in his head. A thought among those thoughts prized enough to win space. A passenger. He wondered if everyone did sleuthing. He wondered if anyone did anything but home renovations and cottage trips. Funerals and grocery shops. Office work and Scentsy parties.

He couldn't find anything on her amongst the flooding articles on tariffs, forest fires, plane crashes, vaccines, feuding celebrity millionaires, or missing men. Nothing on Facebook or any other social media website. Nothing but images of flowers or random women on Google.

He thought about going back to the hospital and asking if he could have her last name, but then the smiling woman in the ad at the side of the page caught his eye. She was a local, apparently. He couldn't imagine that a woman like that lived anywhere nearby, although he had trouble understanding just how big the world really was.

He naturally found himself looking up porn. He didn't even know why; his brain told him to, and he listened. He got up and locked his door. He was about to sit back down but then he caught himself in the mirror. The staring stranger. All he had to do was look away.

"You're delusional," he whispered to himself. "You're weak." He was scared.

"Is that all being a man is... Some muscles and self-confidence? I still have the hormones of a dick that needs a home, don't I?" he said back.

"You used to be strong. You used to be good looking. You didn't give a shit about anything. Now look at you. A soul vampire. Blind and weak, contributing nothing to this world. You are a monster carried on a palanquin. A caged slave. A slave to everyone. Too despicable to please. Too hedonistic to be pleased. You're weak. Weak like a man dragged naked in the dirt. Barren. Scarred. Diminished. Get up!"

He hadn't even realised he'd been crumpling into a thing on the floor. He *was* vermin. A maggot. He curled up and shut his eyes. Lily was all he could see. Lily was all he wanted to see. He couldn't stop saying her name in his head. It was his mantra. Why was he obsessed with everything that touched his mind? She would never remember him.

The gun. Where was the gun? He tripped over himself as he ran for the door.

He was down the street. Where the fuck was the hospital? He stopped at a strip mall he recognized. He ran into the convenience store.

"Hey. Hi. Do you - do you know which way to Queen's Memorial?" he asked the cashier who was sitting behind a shield of glass looking at his phone.

"Hmm? The hospital? Uh...from here, it's about, uh, you have to just go out along the street there. Calvin to Crestford, then take Crestford to the end and turn right on, uh, Eucalyptus. You'll have to take Eucalyptus to Stirling Road. Take your left on Stirling and the hospital is just up Stirling and on the right hand, I think," the cashier described. He dipped his head back down to his phone, satisfied with his own response.

"Thanks," Elgan grunted.

The man tossed a wave in return as Elgan limped back outside. The sky was a grey overcast. New buds shivered on the arms of the trees. A car idled in a parking spot outside the store. A woman sat front passenger side with her head looking down toward her lap. He had an urge to jump in the driver seat and take off, but something in his body seized when he thought of his hands on the steering wheel. He crossed the parking lot to Calvin Street. He tried to keep his eyes averted from the park where he had seen Daniella. D for deadly. A for ambitious.

His limping quickly turned into running. The wind tossed his hair in front of his eyes like a poorly secured toupee.

16

He found the apartment alley dumpster where he'd left his laptop bag, and remnants of his insides that had not completely washed away in the rain. The dumpster hadn't been emptied, but the amount of waste had grown. He looked around and sighed. When he opened the lid, it emitted a vile odour. He took a deep breath and manoeuvred himself inside.

The grime of the dumpster sides stuck to his clothes like tree sap. Each shift of his weight emitted a new puff of rank garbage just as foul as the last. He shifted bags from side to side. One spilled open as he tried to toss it, emptying its guts all over his arms. He ground his teeth in his fury, but his search wasn't in vain as he found the strap of his broken bag and was able to pull it up and out. The gun was tucked untouched inside. He removed it and climbed out.

A woman and her partner walked their dog past the alley. He felt their eyes lock on him as their faces crinkled in unsaid disgust. The pair looked at each other with worried stares and walked quickly onward.

Elgan examined the ebony death dealer. It was empowering. He had to find *her*. Lily. He tucked the pistol into his belt.

He found himself in the shadow of Queen's Memorial. The sun poked through the clouds like an encouraging day-time star. He was going to walk in and ask about her. A woman that perhaps was just of his mind. A woman who may have never existed. Black hair, brown eyes, and a smile that coaxed his soul. No one else could have her. No one else would understand. He had to find her. He entered the hospital.

It was quiet. He found his way back to the mental health ward and faced down the sealed double doors. The concealed safety mocked him. Double doors like pearly gates. She had to be inside. He pressed the buzzer.

"How can we help you?" a masculine voice

inquired.

He tried not to double check the gun against his side like a pulsing heartbeat. He felt a phantom anxiety in his brain. She wasn't going to be there. He was wasting his time. Stupid. This was stupid. He was an idiot. The gun whispered discouraging abuses. What was he supposed to say? Was he supposed to ask for her? Why was he shaking? What was he going to do with the gun? Why was he here?

"Elgan?" Elgan whipped around and saw her. Lily. She was there. She had a worn green backpack slung over one shoulder. A tan jacket. Black shirt, blue jeans, white sneakers. "You came back."

"I...uh-"

"Hi, how can we help you? Are you here as a guest or to be admitted?" the speaker on the wall interrupted.

"You...you want to get out of here?" Elgan asked Lily.

"You don't even know me," she stated with confident surety.

Elgan couldn't look away from her. He didn't want to. "I want to know you. I want to know everything about you."

"This person you think I am is only a shadow. A shadow of yourself. I don't think you should follow me. I don't think you should look for me. Go home. Go to your family."

"You don't understand–"

"I don't want to understand." Her words were like serrated blades across his skin, and yet inspired resilience. He wanted to resist her. He wanted to prove that her power over him was more than just physical lust. "I'm not back here to see you..."

"I didn't say you were. Why are you putting up these walls? Let me help you."

She laughed with a disheartening sadness. A laugh that cut deeper than the serrated edge of her words. He drew closer to her, the pulsing urge of grabbing the pistol at his hip intensified. She put her hand to her nose. "Oh god, you smell terrible."

"I... I was desperate to find something. I had to look in the garbage."

"Did you find it?"

"Yes..." He moved to show her then stopped. "Let's... Let's grab a drink. A coffee maybe? I haven't had caffeine in years, but I... I would love to find a place where we can talk."

She grimaced and brought her eyes to her hands. Hands white as Death's. "You don't know what you're asking..." She seemed momentarily frail and old. Weak and skinny. Pale and cold. It was as if blood didn't run through her, and her body was beginning to show the signs of the weight it placed on her soul. Maybe she needed a doctor. Why else would she be at a hospital? She raised her shoulders with a recovery of will. Her brown eyes drained him, and the pistol's pulses vibrated his bones. "Fine." She took a deep inhale. "Though I warned you, and I will not suffer childish desires. I can't... I can't deal with that."

17

At first, they walked the halls of the hospital in silence. He said nothing, afraid to say the wrong thing. And then she spoke, and when she did, it as if he could hear nothing else:

"I know why you came back. I'm cursed, you know. I'm cursed with the ability to see. I know saying this intrigues you more, but I hate you for that. It doesn't matter if I tell any depraved person that I find them revolting. All they do is laugh like I'm joking. Well, Elgan, I'm *not* joking. I'm not some little girl to be fawned over. I'm not some Shakespearean, doe-eyed Ophelia. I will not suffer some idiot's belief that they own me."

Elgan felt determined to resist her. He'd never felt so desperate to express the truth of his thoughts. "Have you always been this way?"

She looked away for a second and then pulled

his gaze back to hers. "My dad died first. My mom went next. My sister left for California. She may as well be dead too. It all fell apart after my dad died. I was nineteen."

"I don't know what you mean that makes you so cursed. I'm sure most women see people differently than how men do?" Elgan noted, convinced that she had her own identity issues.

"As if you're one to make any assumptions about what *every* female knows or thinks. Based on your puppy dog nature, it appears that you're very lonely. I don't know if you really know what it's like being with a woman. I sense...a deep feeling of self-loathing. Do you disgust yourself? Do you think people are watching you limp around as if you're some kind of beggar? I don't think you have a clue. They'll be reviled by this stench though..."

"I wasn't always like this...whatever *this* is. I'd call myself a cripple, but that sounds very ableist of me. At what point am I socially allowed to comment on being disabled? Anyway, I was in a car accident. I was a bodybuilder. I used to ache to check my muscle pump out in a mirror...but now... The sight of me haunts my mind. Everything I had been was built up within my muscles. Training, suffering, the pain, the callouses, the pump, the looks of desire instead of disgust. I can't even get a job now. I'm a maggot. Special needs people have more dignity in themselves than I do. I'm a reverse butterfly and now I'm trapped in this larva state. My golden years ended behind a steering wheel. I'm junk. I'm no more than the scrap car I wrote off. The hospital, it's my dump and I'm destined for disposal." He didn't know where she was leading them, but they were back at the mental health ward's double doors. "Where are we going?"

She stopped and eyed him for a moment. His body stopped unconsciously. He watched her. He didn't understand why she was staring at him.

"You won't understand at first..." she said softly and turned toward the buzzer. He followed her with his eyes and then rushed quickly after her. He grabbed her wrist before she could buzz in.

"I'm not going back in there. Why are we here?" he panicked.

"I need help... It's not you. It's truly not you.

Leave me here and never look for me again."

He felt the pulsation of death at his side. A steel weight that dragged him deeper into Styx. Knee deep. Charon's toothless grin mocked him. *It would be easier for him to kill her than to forget she ever existed*, he thought manically.

"Don't go back in there," he begged.

She hesitated. An old person with a walker walked past them.

"You don't know what I am," she said softly.

"I trust you."

She laughed. "You're not listening. You have nothing you can offer me."

"What're you afraid of?"

"Hurting you!"

"You can't hurt me. I can't feel anything. I can't feel my toes, my fingers, a woman's warm skin, pleasure, pain. Anything! I'm here by sheer will alone. A ghost clinging to corporeal necessities. I'm not even sure I can feel death. There's nothing you could do that could possibly harm me." Elgan grabbed his own wrist. He dug his uncut nails into his skin. He dug in until blood was dripping off his arm. "You see? I'm a freak in my own way."

Lily stared at the red splatters on the white porcelain. Then she brought her eyes to Elgan's arm. She shivered as she stared at it.

"A car accident?" she whispered.

"Yes. About two years ago."

"I have my own problems... And now you're bleeding... bleeding everywhere. So much blood." Elgan grabbed her by the shoulder as she swayed drunkenly. "A monster. I – I should go." She began to flee, but Elgan grabbed her wrist again. "Stop it! Get off me."

She tried to resist him, but she quickly realized the futility. His grip was a vice that held her in place. His stench suddenly filled his own nostrils, but she barely seemed to flinch.

"I just would like someone to talk to. I'm not trying to force you. I just want you to understand that I can't even feel your skin in mine. "

"I understand," she snapped. "I warned you. I warned you over and over. You insisted this." She slapped him but he was unphased. "I'm Jekyll and Hyde. I'm begging you."

“Come on, just for a small drink and a chat. Your charity for a cripple. A broken man.”

“Fuck… Fine. Fine, but after I'm coming here. I need the rest. I need the escape. There's something horrible inside of me. Something truly terrible.”

Elgan smiled. “It's fine. We can come back after. I'll need to grab my medication anyway.”

He followed her frightened stare back to the blood on the floor. *Was she truly that afraid of him? Another one who saw only a beast?* he wondered.

“Fine,” she stated. She grabbed his bleeding arm. “You should clean yourself up…”

18

The conversation to Elgan was better than what he remembered of sex. A back and forth of intuitive intimacy. They saw each other on chthonic plains, beneath the skin, and beyond the flesh. The conversation swayed like a dance. Elgan was mesmerised. Lily's appalling brilliance made him desperate to hear every word, but that wasn't what made her special: she listened. She watched with eyes that absorbed every word.

She was a loner. Friendless. Loveless. She told Elgan that she was happiest alone, but that there was something in a person's eyes that excited her. Elgan told her about his accident, his surgery, his recovery, and now his own loneliness. He told her of the abuse of an uninterested world. He told her about his disdain for people.

"How can you stand it? The vile stares. The

drooling mouths. They're all animals. Disgusting and rotting. There's no hope for these people..." Elgan said.

"Is there much hope for us? Maybe we're the animals," Lily responded.

"Maybe..."

"What would you do if you discovered that you were the animal? Caged by your own inhibitions. Maybe you shouldn't fear letting out what is inside you. It doesn't have to be some dark secret."

"I can't..."

"Why?" she probed.

She stopped at a streetcar stop and sat down. Elgan sat beside her. The world around him was a blur.

"Where do you live?" he asked.

"Just by Alexandra Park."

"I didn't bring any money."

"You don't have a pass?"

"No, I don't take transit very often. It's dirty, stinks, there's always homeless people, and there's probably bed bugs and roaches."

"I'll pay for you."

When the streetcar arrived, Elgan followed her

on. They sat in a row near the back. She let him sit at the window. The streetcar trundled between walls of construction hoarding and aimless souls with briefcases and black purses. It was strange how empty it was. Empty of life. Towers of stone. A hopeless paradise to slaves. He almost forgot that he was a living embodiment of the city's trash.

He turned and watched Lily. She was looking out the windows on the other side.

"What do you see?" he asked.

"Waste," she stated.

Elgan mouthed the word *waste* and returned to staring out his own window.

After a few stops, Lily stood up and walked casually off the streetcar. He followed her and they walked the busy streets past a cathedral, pissing dogs, and bicyclists who were being honked at by drivers. They walked past Alexandra Park, its sign graffitied, and its grassy fields filled with tents and homeless people. There was a skatepark and a ball hockey arena, both weren't in use, but a lady sat on the bench at the skatepark with her dog and a book.

Lily J-walked to the other side of the street.

God she is beautiful, Elgan thought. He followed her.

She unlocked the side door of a two-story apartment complex and led him inside. They walked down a set of creaky wooden stairs into an open concept basement apartment.

"Sorry it smells stale. I usually burn candles to mask the old building smell, but I've been gone a few days," she said.

Elgan shrugged and removed his shoes at the bottom of the stairs. He noted that it did smell stale, but he figured it couldn't be worse than his own odour. Light from egress windows bathed a rack of plants. He saw the couch and ached to curl into a ball but let her lead.

She led him to a kitchen where she filled a glass of water for each of them from the sink. "Not much else to drink in here... I drank all the wine a few weeks ago."

"No, that's fine." Elgan took a quick swig and watched Lily do the same. "How long have you lived here?"

"Three years."

"Do you work nearby?"

"Not really."

"Do you work at all?"

"Well, I afford this place somehow." She walked over to a stand and turned on music. It was a male pop artist he hadn't heard of before. "Did you like *Harry's House?*"

"I'm not too familiar with it, no. What's Harry's House?"

"You never heard Harry Styles before?"

"No, this is Harry Styles?"

"You're hopeless..."

Elgan laughed. He almost swore for a moment that he felt a strange numbness in his fingertips. Lily smirked slyly. She shook her head then reached into a cabinet above the sink. Elgan turned his attention to a sketch pad on her kitchen table. A naked man was sketched with rough eloquence on the page. He looked as if he was sleeping in the nude. Elgan felt like he recognised the sketched man, but he couldn't quite put his finger on it. Elgan turned the page, and there was the same man drawn. The pictorial man's hands were tied behind his back, and he was kneeling, bowing his head in submission. Elgan flipped to the next drawing, and it was the same man, but he was screaming in apparent agony. Cross-hatching of red was drawn at his feet. An orange and black butterfly was drawn at the corner of the page.

Elgan shut the book and began to say: "Did you dr-"

Lily was beside him before he even realised. Her hands were around his neck. He tried to resist and flail, but she pulled away and was already stepping backward toward a door at the other side of the kitchen. She was smiling, but her eyes were completely dilated. She held a syringe.

"Why did you..." Elgan stumbled forward and had to rebalance himself using the edge of her kitchen counter. His feet became anvils he couldn't lift. He tried to slide forward but collapsed and smashed his head off the table. He tried to blink through the stars that dotted his vision, but everything was spinning. He saw the shape of a monster leaning over him... Lily. Her white smile looked down upon him.

"Shh, shh, shh..."

19

___

When Elgan came to a haze hung over him.

"Mom...?" he mumbled softly. "Mom?" He tried to rub his eyes, but his arms were anchored to his side. "Mommy!?"

"I don't think she's coming for you." A blur stood up from its chair in the corner of the room. "All you know is loneliness."

Clarity shone through the haze and Elgan saw the shadow of the woman. Her face was hideous in its conspicuous disdain.

"You little bitch," Elgan spat. "You goddamn bitch. Why? I would've loved you. I would've given you everything I am. I don't understand."

"You would've given me desperation and disappointment. I don't need you. I never did."

"You're lying," Elgan whimpered. He strained with all his might against the bonds. She had wrapped him in coils of highlighter yellow rope. He was still on the floor, but there were translucent sheets covering everything. "You're just as fucking alone as I am. A lactating cow prowling the psych ward for a man to milk you. You're a wasted nobody. You need a man, don't you? Don't you?!"

Lily put a paring knife to Elgan's throat. She was crying. "You don't know anything. You think you're so smart. You're the dilapidated remains of a bigger man."

Elgan tried to pull away from the blade's edge at his throat. He could only think of his mother. He tried to wrestle to freedom, but it was hopeless. His flaccid body would be a pitiful corpse.

"At least tell me why you're doing this?" he asked in a final plea.

She stood up and started pacing. She mumbled nonsensically to herself. "I have to," she said as she stopped. "I must do this, so you don't hurt anybody else. I must. So – so I don't hurt anyone else. Yes, you'll be my last. You must be my last."

"Who would I hurt? I'm not going to hurt anyone. Please, I don't want to die here."

She stood over him again. She was in her bra and panties. Of all the times he would've begged not to be aroused, this would be the time, but he couldn't stop the pulsating in his groin. A pressure that awoke a sleeping beast. It wanted her. It reached out toward her. It wanted to devour her. It was alive.

"I see it in your eyes. You want me. You don't give a shit about anyone or anything. Human waste." Lily pressed the knife deeper into Elgan's throat. He could feel its edge in a flaring sensation of numbing coldness that pressed against his Adam's apple. "I want out. I need out. You're my ticket to the other side."

Elgan went silent. There wasn't much else for him to do. Trapped again. Pitiful and afraid. He tried to think of a way out, but his mind didn't have the energy to seek it, nor the will. The sensation of feeling was almost blinding. Pinched toes and fingers whined through his limbs. He tried to move his arms and hands again, but they wouldn't budge. His heartbeat was in the crucible of his gut. Thumping, and thumping, and thumping. His chest was on the verge of bursting open. The memory of hands gripped to the steering wheel was in his head He was going to vomit at the memory of it. He should have died that day. He should be dead. That's what was meant to happen. That's what should have happened. Unfortunately, blessings weren't in his deck and now dinner was to be served on the cold edge of a paring knife by some psychotic girl.

A pinch at his side turned into burning.

"What are you doing?! Please don't-don't-don't. Oh god, it burns. It really burns," he cried.

"I can't go back... I can't go back," she cried in harmony with him.

He couldn't bear the sensations that burned across his body, lava leaking from his gut. Whatever tingle had been spurred by his arousal had fell limp. He was beginning to understand he was going to die. The wisdom came over his body like a warm blanket pulled up from his toes to his head. No thoughts, just an understanding. He was finally free. Shock overcame him and whatever momentary sensation he felt had leaked from his body. He prayed that it only leaked from his gut.

It suddenly grew brighter. A light was in his

eyes. A glowing circle of light. She looked down at him with red eyes like brake lights. He attempted to break free, but it was pointless.

The light encompassed him. The pain and pleasure completely gone. His flaccidity returned in a burst of anger, and he forced his phantom muscles to work against the bonds holding him in place.

"I can't feel anything, you stupid bitch. If you're going to kill me then just do it!" he screamed.

She was still crying. "No... No, I need to draw you first. I need to draw you!" She dropped the bloody paring knife to the floor, walked over to her kitchen table and grabbed her sketch pad. She straddled him, pad and pencil in hand. Her erratic movements accompanied by the scratching of a pencil on paper. "How long do you think I can keep you before you die?" She didn't look up from the sketch pad.

Elgan began to laugh. "This must be a real horror show if you're so keen on drawing it. Do you show your drawings to your therapist?"

"I knew this girl once. A gorgeous brunette with big brown eyes and a pixie face," Lily said from behind her sketch pad. "She was always the sweet one. The one everyone was afraid to upset because of her unwavering innocence. The do-nothing-wrong type of girl. As she got older, her blossoming made her even more astonishing. She had big breasts, tight hips, and she never lost the youth of her pixie face." Elgan attempted to force her off him, but whatever sense of athleticism he had regained was not sufficient to budge her. "As she got older, she grew further and further away from reality. A geopolitics specialist and human rights champion whose sole experience in life was being insufferably sweet. A professional con-sumer who believed her shares on Instagram and Facebook alleviated her from being complicit in global atrocities. Grandstanding and gas lighting her way into everyone's inbox as if anything she said was relevant. I hate her." Lily tossed her sketch pad to the side and reached across the floor and grabbed the paring knife. "I hate her!" She stabbed Elgan in the shoulder and jerked the knife out. "I hate her!" She dragged the blade across his chest. Blood spilled everywhere. She stood up and over him, her almost naked body splotched with his blood. "And you know what's funny, Elgan? You want to know the funniest irony... They found her raped and mutilated body outside the Palestinian refugee shelter on Acorn Avenue!"

"And what about the broken men... you've... you've taken. Are we nothing...? Are we... nothing?" Black dots spotted Elgan's vision. "I'm sorry, dad..." He tried to blink through it, but his eyes resisted him. Was he dying? "What a waste..." he mumbled. "What an absolute fucking waste..."

Lily

Lily stared at herself in the mirror. Her face was smeared with blood streaked by her tears. She did it again. She did it again and the relief was like a heaven exploding inside her breast. The sensation shivered up her spine.

But she wasn't free.

The realisation turned her sobs into screams. She yelled at herself repeatedly in the mirror. A nightmare's reflection staring back at her. Hating her. A forest hag feeding on the flesh of the pitiful.

The person upstairs slammed against their floor four times. Lily's heart stopped. She fell on her knees at the toilet. Droplets of salted red created orange ripples in the toilet bowl. She vomited. No one was there to hold her hair back. She vomited again. She struggled to her feet and jumped in the shower.

She relished the scalding heat. She knew that if the cops showed up, she would embrace it in her bloody nakedness.

No one did show up.

Lily set up her easel. Red was her favourite colour, and she knew that this model would take on the red tinting ideally.

She painted it where she had left it: a skinned beast stewing in a pool of its own blood. She had to reposition its arms once and adjust the tilt in its neck, but she was done before the stench began.

She disposed of it when she had cleaned up her paint supplies. Just as she disposed of Austin, Michael, Luke, Alex, Mason, Emerson, Mo, and her first, who she told herself she would never name again. He-who-shall-not-be-named. She would remember all of them. And all of them would remember her as they entered their own eternal hells.

She rolled and bagged the cellophane sheets she had covered the room in. She showered again.

As she brushed her hair after her second shower, her eyes caught themselves in the mirror again. Brown eyes. Black hair like a Babylonian whore.

Was she Lily or Lilith? Only the pitiful would know.

She sat down with a warm chamomile and ticked away at her knitting, finished knit stitching her swatch, ate a bowl of grapes, went to the stairs, bagged the model's dirty runners and garbage-scented clothes, put on her shoes, put on her jacket, grabbed one of the bags and hauled it into the back dumpster. Three more trips would be sufficient. The sky burned orange from the rising sun.

She went back inside, turned on Stranger Things, and fell asleep with knitting needles in her hands and Stevie Nicks on in the background.

End.